Best Wishes
for 2007-Present

George
Fawley

CONTENTS

ACKNOWLEDGEMENTS

Thanks be to God for blessing me with the opportunity to experience first hand the growth season of being tested and tried as described in Psalms 66:10-12. Special thanks to those whose determination of heart worked for my good.

Thanks to the greatest Church family in the world, The Tried Stone Church of Greater Love. Thanks to the members in particular who contributed endless hours of editing, formatting and prayer. Thank God for my son Corinthian Witcher.

DEEDS OF THE FIRST LADY

"SCANDAL ON DIAMOND MINE ROAD"

INTRODUCTION

There are many things that we acquire in life that we actually cherish with our lives. And the thought of loosing these things can hardly be conceived; things such as the house or car of your dreams or perhaps the job that you have studied and worked so hard to get. But in actuality, these things if lost, can be easily replaced. However, there is one thing that is so precious, more precious than any house, car or job and most of us don't pay much attention to it until it is gone. Once you have lost this, you have lost the most valuable thing that you could ever have. You can't buy it, you can't study for it, nor can you sell it. This thing that I am talking about can only be handed down to you by your parents as a result of a gift from God. It is your good name and reputation. Once you have lost it, you have indeed lost something worth crying about. Especially when you have lost it to a vicious attack of slander. One of my favorite proverbs says, *"A good name is rather to be chosen than great riches and loving favor rather than silver and gold,"* (*Proverbs* 22:1). In other words, you can be the poorest lad on the block but if you have a good name to hold onto, you have all that you need. This story is about a young man who lost the most important thing to him because of a vicious attack of slander. He suffered much pain from a community of churchgoers as well as having all of his so-called friends and acquaintances desert him. But little did he know that just as *Romans 8:28 says, "And we know that all things work together for good to them that love God, to them who*

4

are the called according to his purpose," that this attack of slander was indeed bringing about another level of walk in the Lord for him. You see, what this young man did not realize is that the seven years of his suffering, of being persecuted, misunderstood and mistreated was the planting field for a greater anointing in his work for the Lord. Yes a good name is rather to be had than riches or wealth. But if having your good name and reputation marred by a scandal is the way that God chooses to move you into the level of ministry that he has for you, then certainly your latter state will be better than your first. As in the case of Job, God allowed Satan to bring destruction and devastation into the life of this man who was considered a friend of God, a man who walked upright before God, a man who shunned evil. Yet, God who is all-wise and all knowing, allowed the devil to wreak havoc in the life of Job. When we stop and examine this particular book of Old Testament wisdom, it becomes obvious that the suffering of Job, even the defamation of Job's Godly character by his three friends is God's governing and leading hand upon the righteous in the light of the age-old misunderstanding of the sufferings that a righteous man must undergo. It was not until God revealed Himself in His majesty and power (chapter 38-41) that Job, *"perfect and upright"* turned from his own goodness and confessed: *"I detest myself and repent in dust and ashes."* Perhaps you are saying, at this point, *"What does the story of Job have to do with the life of this young man?"*

It has a lot to do with this young man's life and the life of all who are striving to live a life of Godly character. For when we think we are at the optimum of our walk with the Lord, it is usually at this point that God will allow us to be shaken by whatsoever means he chooses in order to bring us face to face with who we are, who God is and where God wants us to be.

CHAPTER I

THE HONEYMOON

The young and talented Reverend Randall S. Whitnall, soon to be the, *Slandered Servant,* would stand all dressed in his pulpit attire on the very top of the outside spiral steps that led into the main sanctuary of this little brick church on Diamond Mine Road. He would stand there greeting each parishioner and seeing the excitement on each face as they hurried inside to get a seat before the place filled to it's capacity. He remembers well, the feeling of being loved and supported by all who would come to hear him preach each Sunday morning. These are his words as he revisits a time and place in his life where there were no regrets.

I could hardly hold back the tears of excitement as I stood there watching such enthusiasm. I must admit, there were times that I would say to myself, *"will this feeling of being loved by so many last, or is this just the beginning of another let down in my life?"* Yet, I was determined to be the best leader that these people had ever had in the history of this Church.

It was in September of 1987, when by a 59 for and 19 against vote, that I was elected to serve as senior pastor of the same congregation where I was presently serving as minister of music. Oh boy, was this an exciting year. Exciting because just three months prior to being elected, my first and only child was born. And two months after being elected, my mother, in whom I loved dearly, went home to be with the Lord. I guess you could say it was a bittersweet year for me. The Church was originally a two family congregation. The Barons and the Whiteheads. The Barons had the voice and the vote, but the Whiteheads had the money. They often fought against each other, but never to the point of dividing or splitting up. They were born and bred on traditional "*old time religion and beliefs*" which by the way left little room for change, even if the bible dictated it. Their basic philosophy was; "*if it was good enough for my mother, then it is good enough for me, without any change.*" I on the other hand was a full-gospel, high-spirited, tongue-talking, foot-stomping, hand clapping, running down the aisles kind of guy. Somehow though, I was able to win their confidence and trust and instituted a lot more changes than I thought could be made. Suddenly, people from all walks of American culture began to flood this place. As each Sunday passed, the crowds grew, the money increased, people's lives were beginning to change and even my marriage of three years had begun to look and feel real good.

The more people joined this little congregation, the less power the two original families had. My first year in office was a real roller coaster of an experience. Though this was my first position of leadership and exciting as it was, I knew that most of the people that were coming to this church were coming with issues that needed to be dealt with. Issues that were not so pleasant. But somehow the Good Lord used me to help a great deal of these people with their issues. The hard work had begun to pay off. In this first year, I received an all-expense paid trip to visit the Land of the Bible, Israel and a visit to Rome Italy was also on the itinerary. Then there was Sister Marion Page, the president of the pastor-aide club. Sister Marion came to Community Church with a lot of experience in aiding church pastors. She became one of my best friends and supporters of the ministry. She was quite charismatic and she used her charisma to influence as many people as she felt necessary to get her job done. Even the board of deacons who thought their position in the church was to pastor the church on their level of thinking, would all melt under sister Marion's influence. However, as appreciative as I was of this woman's work and support of me, before the story ends, she ended up being my worst enemy. She was a two-faced liar and a woman who could manipulate and manage two sets of friends. Time kept her two sets of friends unaware of each other. The one group of friends included others who were members of the pastor's aide club along with myself, my wife and our close friends.

The other group of friends were people who were actually clients of a business that she and her husband ran out of the basement of their home. Further along the way I discovered that the business was selling marijuana. Sister Marion was indeed a good friend, but after the *scandalous deeds of the 1st Lady* took control of the thinking process of the church, she turned against me and stood with those who had purposed in their hearts to get rid of me because of what was being said. In other words as persuasive as she could be at times, she was a woman who could only be a part of the ruling majority, even if the ruling majority was dead wrong. There was a lesson to be learned from Mrs. Page's response to trouble. *"If you don't stand for something, you will fall for anything."* However as the story unfolds in up-coming chapters you will hear more of this notorious woman as she aligns herself with the *"Deeds of the First Lady."*

At this particular time of the new ministry in Community Church, everything seemed to be doing well. Even the minority who had originally voted against me was seemingly at ease. Just keep in mind that the honeymoon was not over. The honeymoon was a period when nobody wanted to see anything or sense anything bad about each other. Just flowing with the tide. Then came the following year and a half of leadership verses followership. That is to say, the main focus of my job was trying to instill in the hearts and minds of the people, the importance of following leadership as the Bible suggests. Most of us in the Church are under the impression that leadership and being a good leader is all that a church needs to be successful. Most of us are even guilty of saying, *" as long as we have a dynamic leader in our church we will go places."* Which is true in a sense. A good or dynamic leader is very important for a church to grow. What is also true is that, in order for a good leader to be successful in church ministry, he or she must have good followers. The mystery of it all is that there is a thin line between leadership and friendship and it is called followership.

CHAPTER II

THE THIN LINE BETWEEN LEADERSHIP AND FRIENDSHIP

As time past, I must admit, even I had a hard time separating the position of leadership from friendship with quite a few people. It was indeed an honest struggle, because of the many people who had appeared to align themselves with me as their new leader. I was young and inexperienced. And it took a while for me to realize that there is a thin line between leadership and friendship. I learned the hard way that a leader is to lead and that a leader who is out to make friends with everybody that he or she comes in contact with is simply setting his self up for disaster. Make no mistake about it; a leader should have at least one person who has been proven to be worthy of being close enough to be called a *"friend of the leader."* Usually that person is someone else who is in a leadership position. Someone who can identify with the trials, troubles and not to mention the heartaches that a leader will experience. The mistake that I made was allowing everybody who seemed nice to get too close to me.

Even Moses, the first leader of God's people, was eventually summoned by God to lead ahead of the people and not with the people. (*Exodus chapter 17),* explains the difficulty of leading among the people. The more time a leader spends leading among the people, the more problems the people will cause. In Moses' case, the people constantly complained to Moses about his leadership strategies and questioned his leadership motives. (Verse #3). So therefore, the Lord said to Moses, *"Go on before the people."* In other words Moses, disconnect your self from their trivial striving that at times appeared to be genuine concerns. Lead in front of them. The distance or line that separates leadership from friendship will give the people that you are leading a better opportunity to follow you as you are leading them. As long as a leader is among the people, there is no space for followship. I am now in my second position as senior pastor and the one thing that I now know how to do is to keep a certain distance in front of the people, not behind, nor among them. Oh, what a difference it makes.

What happened to me in my first pastoral position as a result of allowing too many people to follow too closely to me in the disguise of friends, is that when my day of trouble came, the people that I thought were with me had actually been too close to me and no longer were regarding me as their leader, but as one of their buddies. It is a known fact that good buddies will forsake you when you need them most. My advice to anyone who desires to be a leader is, love the people that you have been called to lead.
Pray without ceasing for everyone who is under your charge. And at times, as situations dictate to do so, fast as well as pray with and for the people. Suffer with the people as they suffer. Rejoice with the people as they rejoice. But do not allow yourself to get too close to the same people that you are trying to lead. There is an anointing upon you as leader that is not upon the people as followers. And because of this anointing, there are things that those who follow cannot understand. Situations that will arise that they who follow cannot handle. Oh yes, there is a thin line between leadership and friendship. That line is called followship.

What is followship? It is the vocation of a Lay-Christian. It is the consciously subjected character that all believers should possess who desires to be a disciple of the Lord. Followship can also be described as being a pursuit to obey an example that has been set. The best leader that any man or woman can possibly be is first preceded by being a great follower. *He, who follows well, leads well.* There have been many sermons preached on the subject of being a great leader. But not as many on the subject of being a great follower. This can be very misleading. For as long as the people of God don't get to hear about the true rewards of being a great follower, it can be easily concluded that the qualities of a great or good leader comes with the title. Not so.

I am reminded of a young man whose followship ability caused him to become the successor of his leader. The 2nd chapter of the book of 2nd Kings tells the story of the great prophet Elijah being translated into heaven in the presence of his faithful servant and minister, Elisha. In the ninth verse of this same chapter, Elijah asked Elisha the question: *"Before I am taken of the Lord what would you have me to do for you?"* Elisha reply was, *"let a double portion of thy spirit be upon me."* As they continued to commune with each other, a chariot and horses of fire came down and separated them and the prophet Elijah was seen no more. But as he was being taken up, his mantle fell and was retrieved by his servant, Elisha. Afterwards, Elisha proceeds with a great leadership ministry in the same power of his master. Verse fourteen states, *"And he took the mantle of Elijah that fell from him and smote the waters and said, where is the Lord God of Elijah? And when he had also smitten the waters, they parted to the one side and to the other and Elisha went over."* In conclusion, Elisha was given the mantel of leadership because of his prior followship character. He willing followed the example set for him.

CHAPTER III

HELP MEET OR HELP MESS

The worst thing that one who is in leadership position can do to his self is to mistakenly choose a *Help Meet*, a partner, a spouse who is not and does not want to team up and be a part of a ministry leadership team. It does not matter if your spouse did not hear the call to ministry. If just one of you heard the call, both of you are to still heed the call into ministry. I can assure you, if one of you received a call from an attorney stating that you will be the heir and recipient to some great fortune, the other spouse would be right there to claim the spouse's part. So then, should the ministry of the Lord be regarded for those of you in the ministry with spouses? Too often I have heard the spouse that did not hear the call make this statement. *"God called him and not me."* Which it to say, I am not doing no more than I have already been doing. My suggestion to anyone with that kind of attitude is this. *Cook, or get out of the kitchen.* Because if you are that determined not be a part of a husband/wife ministry team, then you will be more of a hindrance than a help. It might sound cruel and even unorthodox. But what is the point? What would be the purpose for anybody to stay in a work of the Lord, determined not to work? With that kind of attitude, you have already alienated yourself from the vows of marriage that you took, when you vowed to love and support until separation by death. My final word of encouragement to the spouse who is refusing to step up to the plate, you honestly need to seek God for counsel. I have been in many churches and witnessed the submissive wife trying to pastor the Church with a husband who is determined to be no more than a trustee, usher, or maybe at best, a deacon. Can somebody tell me what is wrong with this picture? I am not by any means against a woman in a pastoral position. But if she has a husband, that man should be willing to step up to the plate and start batting alongside his wife. One more thing: Can anybody explain to me the position of the *First Lady* of the church, without regards to being an active part of the leadership team with her husband? Of course, we all know that this name is to respect and honor the woman who is married to the man who is serving in the position of pastor. Unfortunately too much attention has been placed on this particular title of honor and not enough has been stressed about the duties behind the title. Which is why too many first ladies are under the impression that their job is only to look good.

What then, shall we say to these ministry flaws? If ministry is your calling, particularly leadership and if you desire to have a *Help Meet*, a ministry partner, then by all means seek the guidance and counsel of the Lord. And after you have diligently sought the Lord, just wait for him to place someone in your life. Don't you go looking and picking a mate. Let God do it for you. And then if you are pleased with whom God has picked for you, then it is your choice to accept that person. Remember, Adam did not go looking for Eve. The Bible explains it this way. God caused a deep sleep to overtake Adam. And while he slept, God took a rib from within Adam's body and created Eve. *"And he brought her unto the man."* (Genesis 2:22). Bottom line; trust God to bring you a partner. Because of you go out and get a partner any other way other than God's way, you just might end up with a *Help Mess.*

CHAPTER IV

THE SLANDERED SERVANT
The Story *unfolds*

The story unfolds as I recall, in the third year of leading this congregation that had grown so much in numbers, finances and spiritual maturity. My marriage has now taken a turn for the worst. We have talked on several occasions about going our separate ways. It is lunchtime, on a cool October afternoon. Eva (my wife) called me at work on this particular morning to see if I could meet her for lunch. So I met her at one of our favorite restaurants, which is closer to her job.

"Why do you think we are so unhappy with each other?" she asked me, as we attempted to place our order.

"I am becoming unhappy with you because I am tired of your constant complaining about me" I quickly responded. "You are always accusing me of not loving you. If I didn't love you, I would not have stayed with you these six and half years."

"Yes, I know I complain a lot" she replied, "but I'm beginning to feel as though you care more for that church than you do me. You never tell me that you love me."

"But Eva, how in the world could you even think that I care more for the people in the church than I do my own wife? The problem with you is that you are too insecure, you have always been an insecure woman and no matter how much I tell you that I love you, you are not going to be convinced." As I looked over at her to get a response, I noticed that she had taken her wedding band off and placed on the table close to her unfolded napkin.

"I am just tired of feeling this way," she explained.
"What way, are you talking about?" I said.

"Well I am tired of feeling like you care more for the people in your church family than you do me. All I ever hear from your church members is how much they love you and feel like you really care about them. But I don't hear you say those things to me as often as you get to hear it from you parishioners."

"Eva," I replied, "I am just as tired of hearing you complain about your insecure way of dealing with me as a pastor. If the truth was told and as quiet as it is being kept, you and I both know that the problem is not with the Church. There is something else provoking you into this state of discontentment. You may never tell the truth and I may never find out the truth, but you know that there is more to this than you are telling. By the way, I don't see you making any attempts to make my life at home any better either. You don't clean the house any more; you don't even cook for me. Nor do you wash my clothes. Now here you sit talking to me about my love for you. How much do you really love me? I may not be the perfect husband, but Lord knows I am trying my best to be a good husband to you, a good father to our son and a good leader to our congregation. I really don't know what else I can do. I am here for you at all times. I am always acknowledging my love and appreciation for you in the Church as well as in our home. I am here for you emotionally, spiritually and romantically. Now you tell me, what else do you want me to do? Oh, let's not mention the fact that you have full control of every dime that comes into this house. When you pay the bills and even go shopping for yourself, I never complain. So tell me, what is really bothering you? Why are you so unhappy?" At this point, she stood up, handed me her wedding band and walked out.

"Are you ready to order?" I hear, as I sat in awe, not knowing exactly whether to go after her or just have a quiet lunch all by myself. So I opted to just let her go and to take advantage of a few moments all by myself. I knew that before the day was over, one of us would somehow make an attempt to once again, patch things up. All of this patching on a marriage that had grown sour was actually taking a toll on me. You see, while I was preaching and teaching one thing

*

about family order in the church, my own family was in disarray. And so finally in the spring of the following year, Eva and I came together again and finally decided to call it quits. No more, I had had it with the arguments and accusations. If I was not being accused of loving the Church more than I loved her, I was being accused of wanting to be back in my former lifestyle.

With all the arguing that was going on with Eva and I about nothing that really made any sense, I must admit, there were times that I felt as though my former way of living in sin was more peaceful than the life that I had committed to live with her. However I knew that my life was no longer mine to live as I pleased but to live a life that was pleasing to God. That was my goal. And yet, I knew that I could not continue in a marriage that was not allowing me to do so. Above all things, it was the mystery behind this spirit of discontentment that I was no longer willing to wrestle with. As a matter of fact, I knew that one day the truth would eventually surface. What I didn't know was how cunning and crafty this woman that I was married too could be. You know how it is, when you really fall in love with someone and purpose to spend the rest of your life with that person, you are most of the time blinded from seeing the other side of that individual.

CHAPTER V

I FINALLY DID IT

After much prayer to God for strength and talking it over with Eva, I finally decided to do what I knew would be best for both of us. I also knew that the decision that we had come to would cause a lot of heartaches for a lot of people. But these people, unlike me, were happy in their relationships and marriages. And those who were not so happy were willing to be honest and deal with the problems that were occurring in their marriages. Often I tried to get Eva involved in the local minister's wives conference. I just believed some one in that conference had enough wisdom to help her overcome whatever she was going through. However it was not until I had made up my mind that she suggested going to the conference. I knew it was just an attempt to make it look as if she tried to get help for our marriage.

Eva and I argued much about separation agreements and all the rest of the stuff those goes along with separation/divorce. After we had made up our minds to do it, it seems as though the more I tried to reason with her, the more argumentative she became. By this time I knew that no matter what she would say to me, her arguments were for the purpose of trying to cover up something that she did not want to be uncovered. For one thing, after admitting that for the past two years of being married to me, *her flesh would simply crawl with hate and disgust for me, every day as I would come home from work.* But the closer we came to ending the marriage, the more she wanted to convince me that I was to blame. That somehow I was the one who really wanted out of the marriage. Of course by this time, I was determined to get my peace of mind back. I really didn't care what she would say to me now. What was important to me at this time was, God knew the real truth about what had really taken place in our marriage.

Finally, the day came. It was fourth Sunday in March, when at the end of one the greatest Church services, I announced that there would be a special call meeting after the benediction. I waited until all visitors had left the main sanctuary and then I called the meeting to order. As I stood there, with a letter of resignation laying before me on the podium, I felt an eerie sense of loneliness that I had never felt before, but to my unknowing, would experience for the next seven years to follow. The letter of resignation that I read was two-fold. First, it was for the purpose of informing the congregation of the status of our marriage. And the second purpose was to give these same people who had voted me three years ago, an opportunity to say whether or not they wanted to retain me as their leader. What with all of the fighting and unrest that was in my home and life, along with all of the excitement that was taking place within the church, I forgot that there was a minority group of people, who really did not care for me, but who were following the flow of progress and prosperity that had taken this little congregation to new heights. So guess what? When I stood and read the letter of resignation, it was their day of celebration. On top of it all, the chairman of the board of deacons, the next person in line of authority, was also one of the main people who were just waiting for an opportunity to hit me while I was down. After I had finished reading the resignation, instead of opening the floor for comments and suggestions, he simply rose from his seat with a smile on his face and said, *"This meeting is adjourned until further notice."* Well, at this point, the gates of hell flew wide open and a spirit of slander and disgrace flew into Eva. She quietly slipped out of the meeting, joined herself with some of the younger women of the church who were really shocked at what had taken place. I on the other hand, went out the back door, got into my car and drove to the mountains to weep and find some sort of resolve in all that I had done. After realizing that I had just handed the fate of my career as pastor of this church to the chairman of the board, a mountain retreat was not all that I was going to be wishing for.

However, for the moment, it was the only thing that I could think to do to keep from falling a part. So I drove and drove until I reached a little town in heart of the mountains, not too far from civilization, but far enough to put thinking space between me and the chaos that was brewing in Community Church on Diamond Mind Road.

After calling into my other job and leaving a message in my supervisor's voicemail letting him know that I would not be coming into work on Monday morning, I spent a total of one night and a day just relaxing and thinking about what had happened, what was going on while I was away and what would take place in my life in the future. I knew Community Church was hurting, but I had to be honest about what was going on in my marriage.

After being absent from civilization for a day and a half, I finally got my little overnight bag packed, checked out of the motel and began driving back down the mountain to get on the interstate that would take me home. I really was not looking forward to being in the same house with Eva, my wife; however, I missed my son Joshua, very much. So I was really excited about getting home to see him. Sure enough, as I stuck my key in the door, I heard his little feet running down the hallway. As I entered the door, he leaped into my arms. As we were embracing each other, he began to ask me about where I had been. I just simply smiled and said to him, *"daddy had to go away for a little while."* It was then that Eva cleared her throat as a gesture of disgust and disapproval of my presence. She then got up from where she was sitting in the living room watching TV and went into the bedroom and slammed the door. I guess in an attempt to let me know that I had to sleep in the room with Josh. Which was just fine with me because I had no intentions of sleeping in the same bed with her again.

Just before I decided to turn the TV off and attempt to go to sleep, the telephone rang and before I could grab it, Eva had picked it up. So I just lay there resting and just before I fell off to sleep, she stuck her head in the door and said, "Pick up the telephone." So I reached over and picked up the phone and said "Hello," to my surprise it was her mother on the other end.

"What's up Mary Lou," I said.

She replied, "Randall I just wanted to let you know that Eva has told me all about you all splitting up and you need to know that I am not upset with you. I had a feeling that you two were not going to make it. We all know how stubborn Eva can be. Both of you are just so different from each other. All I ask of you is to promise me that you two will remain friends for the sake of my grandson."

"Mary Lou, that goes without saying," I replied. "We have to be civil for his sake. So don't worry, I promise you we will do our best to be civil for the sake of Joshua. We both love him dearly."
"All right then, take care of yourself Randall, you have been a good man to my daughter."
"Good night Mary Lou." I said and hung up the phone.

So for the next week, I bunked out in the room with Josh, conversed with her only when it was necessary and spent as much time away from the house as possible each day so that I would not have to face her. For some odd reason, since our separation has become public knowledge Eva seems to a much happier woman. Several times I caught her with a strange smile on her face. This I could not figure out. Finding ways to keep a distance between the two of us until I moved out was all that I could handle during this time.

CHAPTER VI

A GOOD NAME IS BETTER THAN NO NAME AT ALL

One week had past, I was still living in the same house with Eva and our son, but all the while making plans to move in with my sister until I could find a place to rent. Suddenly, I began to receive phone messages from different people in the Church, suggesting that I come back to clear up some questionable things about me that were spreading throughout the congregation and community. Mrs. Esther Baron, one of the seniors of the church and a dear friend, who also was my son's nanny, was one of the concerned people who had called. I didn't bother to call her back; I simply got into my car and paid her a visit. As I stood there on her doorstep, waiting for someone to open up, I became afraid of what I might hear from Mrs. Baron.

"Hello, Mrs. Bee!" I yelled out, since I could see her peeping through the curtains. As she opened the door, she broke down and began to cry. I hugged her and started crying as well, not really knowing the pain that she was experiencing. But we both sat together on the couch and finally pulled ourselves together.

"Rev. Whitnall, do you have any idea what is being said about you in the Church?"

"No, I don't, but please tell me what's going on."

"Well," she started, "about two days after you left the Church, some of the younger women of the congregation had a meeting with the board of deacons. They told the board, your wife, Mrs. Whitnall had met with them on the same Sunday that you resigned and told them that you were not being truthful about why the two of you decided to go your separate ways. Now Reverend, you know as well as I do that Brother Phil Baron, our Chairman, didn't care that much for you anyway. And what they continued to tell him just made his day."

"Go on Mrs. Baron," I said.

"Well, Sister Lynette Brocks, Sister Ophelia Laurese, along with Ms. Hathaway, the pianist, continued to tell the board that the real reason you all decided to divorce was because you had gone back to your old lifestyle and that your wife had caught you in the bed with another man! Now Reverend, you need to know that me and my husband and our whole family love you dearly and no matter what has happen you can count on us for support. Just tell me that it's not true."

At this point my heart was in my mouth and all I could do was shake my head in sorrow and say, "no ma'am, its not true. She is the biggest liar and she is not going to stop until she has turned everybody against me! Now I understand why she has been walking around the house with that big smile on her face. She knows that this is just the kind of dirty deed that would actually ruin my chances of ever being reinstated into the pastorate at Community Church."

"But why Reverend would she do such a thing?"

"Mrs. Baron, you've got to understand, this woman that is my wife is not a happy woman. She is miserable and will make anybody who comes in contact with her the same way. I don't know what to do. Because I know that if she has convinced a few with her lies, she has convinced many."

"What do you mean by many, Reverend Whitnall?"

"I simply mean that she has gotten to the hearts of many people by now. You see, Mrs. Baron, this is not the first time that we have split up. What those people at the Church don't realize is, this is my second time around with her. We separated after the first year of our marriage. As a matter of fact, it was about four months after we had moved into this area of the state. It basically all began the same way. Out of nowhere she started arguing with me about the smallest of things. We had not united with any church at that time. As a matter of fact, the only people we knew in this crowded area were my sister and her family, which was where we were living at the time. Everything was so much different here than where we used to live. We both were working two jobs trying to save enough money to buy a home as quickly as possible so that we would not have to live with my sister and her family too long. Her complaint with me then was that I didn't spend enough time with her. Working two jobs did not leave a whole lot of time for us to spend with each other. The weekends were the only time that we spent with each other. And she knew that this was just a temporary thing. The real problem, which is something that she does not want any of her family to know is that after being married for a year, she realized that she was not ready to settle down in a marriage with me or any one else. So eventually, Mrs. Bee, I got tired of her fussing with me about nothing and she got tired of me because I was not falling for her game. So right there in my sister's house, we called it quits. She moved out and I finally rented a condo with the money that I had been saving. However, it was not long after we had gone our separate ways that my mother started calling me telling me that I needed to come home and straighten out these ugly rumors that were circulating about me. The rumors were the same as now. And for a long time I could not bring myself to believe that Eva was the one who started the rumors. But eventually I found out. While on a trip that the two of us made back home together to explain to our parents individually why we were no longer together. She was visiting with her family when she explained to them that the reason for our separation was that she had caught me in the bed with another man. It didn't cause me half as much pain as it's going to cause this time. You see, last time I was not pastoring or in any leadership position. So it didn't do much destruction. But now, my name is known all over this county as being the Diamond Mine Road Pastor. The one thing that my father gave me that is more precious than silver and gold is my name. And now, the devil is out to destroy that!"

We both hung our heads and began to weep again. "But why Reverend, would she accuse you of being with another man?" Mrs. Baron asked.

"Well, Mrs. Bee before I explain to you her reason for saying that I was with another man let me ask you this question. Did anybody happen to ask her who this other person was?"

23

"No, not to my knowledge" Mrs. Bee replied, "just another man."

"Okay, Mrs. Baron, I truly believe that I can trust you with my life, so I am going to tell you the real reason why her story is told the way it is. You see Mrs. Bee, when I was a younger man, as early as my late teens and certainly before I gave my life to the Lord, I experienced many things."

"What kind of things are you talking about Reverend?"

"Well you know that I hung out with all kinds of people. In other words, Mrs. Bee, I also hung out with the gay crowd. I had quite a few gay friends male as well as female. But after God gave me a renewed sense of values and purpose, I was set free from the bondage of such wayward ways. So when I met my wife, Eva, and after we had been dating for a while, I thought it would be wise to let her know from whence I had come. I just thought being honest with her would be the best thing to do. But it ended up being the worst thing that I could have ever done. Because whenever she couldn't have her way, whether it was financially or sexually, if you get my drift, my past is what she would throw up in my face. I was constantly reminded of where the Lord had brought me from. Now she is using it to cover her tracks of revenge again. So now you have the whole truth and nothing but the truth. Unfortunately, those who have been poisoned by her treachery will never believe the truth, not coming from me. Mrs. Bee just keep me in your prayers, that God will give me the strength to endue the awful days that are coming my way."

"I will Reverend Whitnall. Just take good care of yourself and be careful."

"Thanks Mrs. Bee. God bless you and your sweet family. There is one more thing that you need to know Mrs. Bee."

"What's that Reverend?"

"She's going to use whomever she can to help her take me down. So be watchful."

"Reverend, you don't have to worry about me. Just let her come to me. I will be waiting and ready for her." As I was about to reach for the door knob, Mrs. Bee's husband, Deacon Jerome Baron, the oldest member of the board, came through the door with such a disgusting look on his face.

"Good afternoon Deacon Baron," I said. "You look like you have seen a ghost."

"Well son, I have not seen a ghost, but I just came from a spooky board meeting that turned out to be a Randall S. Whitnall barbecue."

"Well deacon, I don't have time right now to go into details, but your wife will fill you in on what is really going on. Right now I've got a meeting with the devil himself. So take care. I'll see you later."

"Oh by the way Reverend, you'll be getting a call from the chairman. It seems as though they want to meet with you tomorrow night if possible, to find out what's really going on with you and your wife."

"Thanks deacon, I will be there at seven-thirty sharp. I just hope to God they are not falling for this mess."

"Well Pastor, whatever has happened to cause this kind of uproar in the Church must be really serious."

"Like I said Deacon, your wife will explain to you what is going on. I really have to run. But I will be at the meeting on tomorrow night."

CHAPTER VII

CONFRONTING THE DEVIL

I could hardly see the road as I sped home to confront Eva about this evil she had inflicted upon me again. Pulling into the driveway I saw her looking out of the kitchen window and as son as she noticed me pulling up, she retreated back into the living room. It's moments like these that you wish your house had the same kind of doors that the supermarkets have. You know the doors that open automatically. As I rushed into the house, she was in the living room pretending to be watching the television. I immediately grabbed the remote and turned the TV off. As I turned to her, she began to look up at me with a smile on her face and said with boldness, "you ain't seen nothing yet!"

"Eva," I said, "just tell me why in the world did you have to do such evil against me? Before you answer, let me inform you that I just spent the last two hours at Mrs. Baron's house listening to her tell me about the mess that you've started. I also stopped by Sister Page's house to see if she had heard anything. And of course she had. She also told me that you are also telling people that you still love your husband. How in the world could you love me and do this kind of evil? Woman, you don't have a clue about what it takes to love someone!"

"Just shut up Randall!!" She blurted out. "You should have known better than to think I was going to stand by and watch you ride off into the sunset without having to pay for making my life miserable. Oh, by the way, your friend and pastor's aide lady, Sister Marion Page is confirming my story. So you'd better be careful what you say around her. It seems as though you dared to trust this lady with the secrets of your past. The only thing that I am doing is going before her to plant a seed that eventually she will have to verify. And another thing, I found out that your pastor's aide lady and her husband have quite a *lucrative* business going on in their house."

"What kind of business are you talking about?" I asked.

"It seems as though their house is where you can buy some of the best marijuana and other drugs I guess. But you ought to know, since you all are such good friends. I would think she would confide in you like you confide in her."

"But Eva," I said, "Do you have any idea that you are using my past to destroy me. The only reason that I shared my past experiences with Mrs. Page is because she came to me with a concern about a good friend of hers whom she had discovered was in this kind of lifestyle. So as an attempt to let her know the possibilities of her friend being set free from this bondage, I shared with her what God had done for me. If Mrs. Page is saying anything, which I truly don't believe, she is only repeating what you have already told her."

"Randall, all I know is this, my life was better before I married you. But since I married you, my life has become a mess."

"Your life was messed up when I met you Eva. Because of all the physical abuse you suffered from the hands of your mother as a little girl and now you have the nerve to say that I made your life miserable! Don't you ever forget about how you just cried your heart out as you were telling me how your mother used to whip you so hard with belts and switches and how she would put you in another room all by yourself and dare you to come out until you had stop crying. This kind of treatment was inflicted upon you all during your childhood and now here you are today, almost twenty years later, suffering from severe insecurity. Before you say another word to me about not loving you, you need to make sure that you understand that it's not my love that you should be questioning. I have done everything in my power to show you how much I love and care for you. Many times I have proposed to you the idea of going with you to talk to a professional about this. But every time you would blow my head off with such a fit of anger, screaming to me that you don't need any help. I tell you this one thing, you might destroy my name and good reputation for a season, but you will be the one who will suffer in the end!"

It was at that very moment that I realized I had to pack what little stuff I could, throw it into the trunk of my car and first thing the next morning get out of this house before I lost control of my temper and hurt this evil witch.

The last night I spent in the same house with her was indeed a nightmare. I have never argued with anybody before as much as I argued with her. Finally, just before I decided to go to bed to get some rest, I remembered to ask her about who this other man was. "Who are you saying you caught me in the bed with Eva?"

"Your good friend, Brother Otis Henley."

"How could you do this to a man that neither one of us really knows. Of course, you know his wife."

"Now I see why you and her have become such good friends in such a little time. You saw a good candidate to use for your selfish plot against me. As a matter of fact, Brother Henley has not been in the Church long enough for you to even think such. So I suppose you are telling his wife, your supposed best friend, that your husband and her husband have got a thing going on."

"Well, who knows?" She shouted back. "Seems to me that you two have been spending a lot of time together lately. It just all adds up Randall. You two have so much in common."

"And just how do you figure that?"

"Well according to his wife, he used to do some of those same things that you used to do. And besides, he looks like *the type*."

"You are a sick young woman, Eva. It is a shame you don't care about anybody's happiness but your own. I will be leaving in the morning and sometime tomorrow afternoon I will be picking up the baby from Sister Page's house."

"You just make sure you bring him back here to me. He needs to be with his mother during these times."

"Yeah, right! The boy needs to be with you about as much as I need a hole in my head."

"We'll just see what the courts have to say about that now won't we?"

"Just shut up Eva!! I am simply too tired to listen to any more of your big mouth!!" That night I slept with one eye opened. It really wasn't a good sleep at all. The next morning, which was Saturday, I got up packing to get out of that house. After about four hours of trying to stuff every thing that I could into the trunk and back seat of my car, I was finally ready to leave this nightmare behind. It was a rather warm spring morning; Eva had gotten up and gone into work so that she wouldn't have to see my face. This was of course, a mutual feeling. If it wasn't for having a child with this woman, I could easily erase her from my memory. What a joke.

It was about twelve noon, my car was all packed and I was just about to pull off to go live with my sister until I found a place of my own, when suddenly I hear this little voice saying to me, *"you have forgotten something."* So with much regret I began to look in the back seat to see if every thing that I had packed was there. I even got out and examined the trunk of my car. I was quite certain that I had every thing that I needed. Nevertheless, to satisfy this little voice in my head, I went back inside to check the house one last time. As I began to put the key into the door, I could hear the telephone ringing. So, I rushed into the hallway, picked up the phone and said hello. The voice on the other end was that of a preacher friend of mine who had become a good friend of Eva's as well. I had not heard from him in over a year, so I was quite shocked to hear from him on the day of my separating from Eva.

"What's up Israel?" I said.

"Oh I am doing just fine Randall. Is Eva there?"

"Uh, no, she isn't. So have you gotten married since the last time we saw you?"

"No, I sure haven't. Do you know where Eva is?"

"Why are you so concerned about Eva?" I asked.

"No particular reason" Israel replied.

"She is supposed to be working today. Would you like her number?"

"Oh no, that's all right Randall I have her work number right here. I'll call her there."

"Okay, bye." As I hung up the phone and began to make my last exit, I finally realized what the wedge was, or I should say *who* the wedge was that had come between Eva and I. Israel had been a friend of mine for a number of years. We met at a Christian musicians workshop that was held at the local community center not far from where we lived. Both of us were guest musicians participating on the program. So naturally Israel became a friend of the family. Quite often he would stop by for fellowship and dinner with us on Sunday evenings. Then all of a sudden, he just dropped out of sight. After many attempts were made to contact him, I finally gave up, concluding that maybe he had moved out of town. But going back into the house intending to make a last search for things that I had intended to take only convinced me of why I had not seen or heard from Israel in such a long time. Not to mention the fact that he had a reputation of being a lady's man. Quite frankly, I knew of several women in Community Church who would give their right arm to date him. It also explains why every time I would mention Israel's name, or try to contact him, Eva would appear to be so nervous. She would always try to appease my curiosity of his whereabouts by saying, "*Don't worry about him. I'm sure you will hear from him when he is ready for you to hear from him.*" Well, I'm sure he wasn't ready for me to hear from him, not today. To satisfy my curiosity, I scanned the house one more time to make sure I had not left anything. As I entered the master bedroom, I notice that the top right drawer of the chest of drawers where Eva kept a lot of papers was not shut completely. So I simply stepped over to the drawer and made an attempt to push the papers down into the drawer and close it when I noticed that what I was pushing down was a stack of bank deposit slips. Out of curiosity I examined the deposit slips only to find that they were deposit slips from a checking account that I knew nothing about. The slips dated back as far as a year. Most of the deposits were made bi-weekly, with most of the week's deposits totaling as much as eight hundred dollars. I then realized that the little voice in my head, telling me that I had forgotten something, was an angel revealing to me other evil deeds of this woman that I was married to. Now I know why so many times our joint checking account was overdrawn. I knew that there was enough money coming into the house to take care of the little bills that we had. Eva would always come up with some reason for the overdrafts. But it was I who had to put more money back into the account to cover everything. I concluded there was no need to cry over milk that has already been spilled. Because once I get out of this, she won't have the opportunity to do me this way again.

As I backed out of the driveway, there was one thing that stuck in the back of my mind. This so called friend of mine, Israel, calls my house on the day that I am moving out, asking to speak to my wife and not having much to say to me except, *"I know her number at work."* Well, I really could be upset about the whole thing, but I am so determined to get away from this two-timing, backstabbing, deceiving woman, I really don't care. I hope she treats him better than she did me. But then again I know that reality says, *"What goes around, will come around."* All I want at this point is my peace of mind and the opportunity to let people see for themselves the kind of liar and deceiver I have been living and struggling with for these past seven years. Even if nobody finds out the truth about Eva, what is most important is knowing that I know the truth, she knows the truth and above all the God that I serve knows the truth.

CHAPTER VIII

THE MOTIVE AND THE MISTAKE

About two weeks has gone by and although sleeping on the sofa of my sister's tiny one bedroom apartment is definitely not a long term plan of mine, it is however, worth it all, just being away from the misery that I had lived with for so long. Nevertheless, I must admit that I am very curious to know what gain does my wife expect to get from all of this treachery. Just how far is she going to take this?

It was about six o'clock in the morning as I stepped out of the shower to get dressed for work, my sister Darlene yells to me from her bedroom, *"telephone."* As I stepped into the kitchen to pick up the phone, Darlene looks at me and says with a quiet voice, *"it sounds like one of the ladies from the church."*

"Hello," I said.

"Good morning Reverend, sorry for calling so early." The voice on the other end said.

"No, it's okay. I'm up getting dressed. Who is calling? Sister Henley, is this you?"

"Yes Reverend, it is. I need to talk to you whenever you have the time."

"Well, right now I am not on the Church schedule, so most any time will be alright with me."

"Reverend, what about meeting me this evening around five, at the Golden Kettle restaurant on main street."

"That will be just fine, See you then." I hung the phone wondering what this meeting was going to be about. However, I just put it to rest knowing I could not afford to spend the day at work wondering about something that I had no clue about. So I patiently waited and worked my way through the day until I found myself sitting in the parking lot of the restaurant one hour ahead of schedule. As I sat waiting, my heart began to rejoice as I thought about my plans for the weekend. I had not been to Church in two weeks, so I knew that come Sunday morning that was where I wanted to be. In the house of the Lord, where I knew I could find some sense of comfort and joy. I could almost hear the choir as they marched down to the aisle into the choir loft singing one of my favorites, *Worship the Lord.*

I got tired of sitting in the car, so I decided to go inside and wait out the remaining ten minutes. Just then, I saw Mrs. Henley pulling into the parking lot, so I walked over to greet her and walk with her into the restaurant.

"Praise the Lord and good evening sister Henley." I said.
"Praise Him, Reverend. I am glad you could make it at such short notice. Come on, let's go in and get a bite to eat." As we were being seated, I right away asked the question,
"What is this meeting all about?"
Without any hesitation she began, "It's about, you, my husband, myself and the games that people play. Reverend Whitnall, as you well know, my husband and I split up about a month ago."
"Yes, I am aware, please allow me to say how sorry I am that it happened. I am sure by now you have heard about my wife and I going through the same thing."
"Well, yes. That is exactly what I wanted to talk to you about. Your wife is playing games with our lives."
"What do you mean?" I asked with much curiosity.
"Well, as you know, you and my husband have been targeted as being two men who left your wives because of your love for each other."
"Yes I am aware of what Eva has been broadcasting. I am just not clear why she chose to involve you and your husband. Of all the people to use, it is really baffling me why she would use you, her closest friend."
"Well Reverend let me explain. But first let me ask you this question. Did you ever wander how and why we became such good friends in such short time?"

"Yes I did wander, but then it seemed as though God put you in my wife's path to be a comfort to each other as young Christian women do from time to time."

"Well that's what I thought too. You see I never had any women of the church to take such an interest in my life as your wife did. She simply knew how to encourage me and make me feel as though I really mattered in the church. I just felt so comfortable talking with her. So comfortable that I shared with her all about the ups and downs of my marriage to Otis. She knew the right words to say to me to help me deal with my situations. If it had not been for her support I would not be where I am now in my walk with the Lord. But then, there was one thing that she kept asking me about."

"What was that, sister Henley?"

"One day she invited me to go with her to the mall. We shopped and dined sufficiently, thanks to your master card. Anyway, as we began to sit down to dinner, I began to talk about my marriage, my husband and what I perceived as the problem with our marriage. She was so consoling, so encouraging, I just felt that I could tell her any thing. So I did. I talked to her about my opinion of my husbands past lifestyle and how I thought it was affecting our marriage. It was like I had opened a bag of her favorite candy. She just dove in and started asking me all kinds of question. By the time we had finished dinner, I felt a sense of relief and yet I felt like I had exposed my own nakedness. But of course, she knew the right words to say to me to make me feel like I had done no wrong."

"Wait a minute sister Henley. Let's back up and talk about what exactly it was that you told Eva."

"Well Reverend, I really do regret ever saying this to your wife. I guess after not really finding anything else to blame for our cold bedroom, I just imagined that it was something from my husband's past that he didn't want to talk about."

"Hold it. So you just assumed that it was what?"

"I just assumed that it was my husband's lifestyle before he met me while he was in the Navy. It was a gay lifestyle."

"So you just imagined something like this about your husband! Did he ever tell you such?"

"No Reverend he never told me anything of the sort. It was all an assumption. Reverend I am so sorry."

"Sorry for what?" I asked her.

"Sorry for just being so stupid. I need to get something else off of my chest. I need to tell the whole truth to somebody and I can't think of a better person to talk too than you."

"Well Mrs. Henley" I said, "if it's gonna make you feel any better; I am here to listen to what ever you feel the need to say." As I looked up from my cup of coffee to glance at Mrs. Henley, she became overwhelmed with tears.

"Please excuse me Reverend; I just can't help myself right now. But anyway, what I want to say to you, I have already confessed in a meeting that I was called into with your sister and her husband. I am surprised she has not told you."

"Sweetheart" I replied, "I have not had the time nor have I been in the right frame of mind to call my sister or any other members of my family."

"Well this is what I need to confess to you, Reverend. The reason I have been so upset with Otis and the reason that I have been trying to make Otis look bad is not because of any assumption that I had of him, but because of something that I did, that I have been trying to cover up. You see Reverend; our marriage has been on the rocks for more than a year now. Also during those rocky times, we have just been sharing the same house for the sake of our child. All of this time we have been sleeping in separate rooms of the house. So I am sure you can understand how lonely this kind of living can be."

"Well I suppose I can." I replied.

"Anyway, Reverend, I was tempted and I yielded to a temptation to contact my last boyfriend before Otis. We met for dinner twice and then he invited me over to his house the third time. Things got a little out of hand. We slept together that night and six weeks later I found out that I was pregnant."

"So how did you handle that?" I asked

"Well I didn't handle it the way that I should have, which is why two years later I am still very much convicted. The only person that I told was my mother. So she gave me the money and set up the appointment for me."

"What kind of an appointment?"

"It was an appointment with the county women's clinic for an abortion. Reverend I had an abortion and I dared not tell Otis, even about getting pregnant. After all, we had been sleeping in separate beds for close to a year. What do you think he would have done?"

"Well I really don't know your husband that well to even try and imagine what he would have done." I replied.

"It really doesn't matter now that we are in the process of divorcing. Life goes on. And we just have to learn how to go on with our lives. Anyway the biggest mistake that I made had nothing to do with me concealing my pregnancy and abortion from Otis. It was telling your wife about all that had happened to me and my assumptions about my husband. I never knew anyone who could be so vicious as your wife, Eva. It was the biggest mistake that I could have ever made."

"Well Mrs. Henley, it may be unfortunate for you and I am truly sorry for the way that this has turned out for you. But let me assure you, this information has cleared up one important thing that I didn't quite understand. Which is, why she chose to use your husband as a part of her escape plan."

"Reverend I have something else that I must confess."

"What is that?" I said.

"Well, I knew all about you and your wife's separation before you did."

"For some reason I can believe this. So tell me, how did you find out?"

"Even though I shared a lot of personal things with Eva, there were times when she would tell me things about her marriage, such as her intent to leave you one day."

"But why was she so unhappy being married to me? Can you explain that?"

"I will try. This is what she told me. She just simply did not want to be a pastor's wife. As long as you were just an associate minister of the church, it was alright with her. Even with you being the minister of music, she could deal with that. But once you were elected to the pastorate of the church, she just couldn't deal with that. She said that people expected too much out of her as the first lady of the church. She would have left you a long time ago, but she had to wait until she could get her hands on the right amount of money and a new car. She got the new car, the problem was, you didn't give her enough time to get the right amount of money that she wanted. So her attempt to destroy your name and reputation was revenge for moving too fast. She had been planning her escape for a long time."

"Well Sister Henley" I said, "I wish she had not used your husband. The few times that he and I hung out together while you and Eva went shopping, just gave me a good impression about your husband's personality. He really doesn't deserve to be caught up in this mess and neither do you."

After listening to all that Sister Henley had to say, I no longer felt hungry. All I wanted to do was go somewhere and cry my eyeballs out. Eventually before I got back to the apartment, I had done just that. The only regret that I had in hearing the truth is, if I had known sooner that I was married to a woman who had been planning my demise for the past year, I would have left sooner. However, I knew that I had to give the marriage my best shot before throwing in the towel. I concluded that, Eva's motive for destruction could have work for her, but her mistake was, telling the person that she had abused, misused and deceived. My goodness, this is what you call, *deceiving without a clue.* This was the beginning to be quite an eventful Friday evening. I wondered how eventful will this meeting with the board of deacons would be? I guess I will soon find out.

CHAPTER IX

MEETING WITH THE BOARD

All eyes were fixed on me as I came into the room where all of the good brother deacons were sitting. As soon as I sat down, Deacon Phil Baron, the chairman, called the meeting to order and proceeded to give a statement of the occasion. "Brother deacons", he said. "We are here to get to the bottom of the confusion that is now surfacing from the marriage separation of Reverend Whitnall and his wife. As you all know since the Reverend came before the Church offering his position as pastor to be reconsidered, certain young women of the Church have come forward with some questionable things surrounding the reason for this split between the Reverend and his wife. Now to you Reverend Whitnall, I need to inform you that before this rumor started circulating, we the board had a meeting with your wife to find out in the event that the church body decides to retain you as their pastor if she would have any problems with the decision. She told us that we didn't have to worry about a thing. She had no intentions of causing any problems if you are retained. She did state that the separation was a mutual agreement between you two."

"Hold it brother chairman!" I declared. "If she has told you this, then what is this meeting all about? What exactly have I been called to this meeting for?"

"Well Reverend Whitnall, what we the members of this board would like to know is what are you going to do about your marriage?"

"Just what do you mean?" I asked. "What does anybody do when they have done all that they know to do to hold a relationship together and it still falls apart? What is this board looking for me to tell them? A lie or the truth? I am not going to lie to this board about my situation just so I can have your favor. In other words if you are looking for me to promise you that my wife and I will be getting back together just to satisfy your personal desire, then you are mistaken. I cannot make this kind of promise to you. I really don't know myself what the outcome of my marital situation will be. I can only truthfully talk about what has happened and what is going on now. So if you will give me a moment, I will attempt to let you know exactly what is going on. For starters, my wife and I have both concluded and agreed that happiness for us is going our separate ways. For almost a year now we have wrestled with making this decision. We are just not happy with each other for reasons that I really don't want to go into. If I were to tell you everything that has been going on between the two of us, then I will be forced to say things about Eva behind her back, that probably will be misunderstood. I refuse to do that. But I will tell you this, if you all will be patient and wait before you write me off, I can guarantee you, the truth will surface and then you will be able to understand why we are no longer together. Listen brother deacons here is something that is personal that I want to share with you, something that I felt was not necessary to share with you while I was serving you as pastor because it is something that took place before I even came to Community Church. You see, my wife and I had separated for a year, which was just before I was elected as pastor. And doing that one-year that we were separated, the same rumors started to circulate. And it was because Eva was challenged by her family and she felt that a story like this would help appease her family in accepting the reality of her marriage being broken up."

"I have a question." Came a voice from the back of the room. It was deacon Curtis Langley.

"What is the question?" I asked.

"If your wife and you had been separated before and she took it upon herself to slander your name like that, why did you go back with her?"

"Well deacon," I said. "I have been asked that question many times. But to tell you the truth, I felt led of the Lord to give my marriage one more try. I guess I wanted to make sure that I had done all that I could do to make things better before throwing in the towel for the last time."

"So you are telling us that Mrs. Whitnall is spreading these rumors about you to appease her family again?" Asked Deacon Langley.

"No, not this time. She is using this slanderous attempt because it worked for her before. Only this time she is doing it to cover up something that she doesn't want anybody to see right now."

"Well what is that?" Asked one of the other deacons.

"At this moment I stood up and said, that's enough! I will not go there with you. But as I said before, if you just watch and wait, you will see for yourself." As I looked around at the other members of the board, Deacon Lester Good raised his hand to ask a question.

"Brother chairman and other board members, I would like to suggest that we give the church body and opportunity to talk this over with the Pastor, because it is really the membership who will cast the deciding vote."

"Deacon Good," came the voice of the chairman, "all I want for the Reverend to know that he came here with a wife and in order for him to stay here and continue serving this church as pastor, he needs to be with his wife."

"Brother chairman," I said. "Is this your personal opinion, or are you speaking for the Church?"

"It really doesn't matter Reverend, but if you must know, yes. Any pastor of mine has to be married."

"I see now where this is going, straight to nowhere." I replied. "This is really all about you and what you want and not what the Church wants. Am I right deacon?" I asked.

"Again, if you really want to know the truth, I never believed the rumors anyway, replied the chairman. This issue is not about a rumor that has surfaced because your wife is trying to cover up something or revenge, but it is about you and the possibility of you being pastor without a wife." Before I could comment any further deacon Richard Jones stood on his feet and offered a motioned to have a meeting with the church to hear the church's opinion.

"Before this motion is acted upon I said, let me ask this question. Will I be notified about the meeting? I truly want to be there."

"Reverend, what we will do is start announcing to the church this Sunday that a meeting will be scheduled for the following Sunday after services. This will give anybody who may not be in service this Sunday an opportunity to be informed about the meeting being held next

Sunday after service. If this is alright with the other members of the board." The remaining members unanimously gave consent. "And by the way Reverend, please leave me your telephone number where you are living so that I can call you and remind you of the meeting." As the motion was being acted upon and the meeting was adjourned, I wrote down the telephone number to where I was living with my sister, the telephone number at my job and the telephone number of Ellen, my other sister who lives two blocks from my job. As I left the room, I handed the information to the chairman and said, "Have a good evening."

CHAPTER X

TWO SNAKES
"THE RUMOR AND THE RUNNER"

      One week had past. It was Friday evening again and as I was leaving work I decided to go by and visit with my sister Ellen and her family. As I pulled into the driveway, Ellen's husband Abner was in the yard working. When he looked up and saw me getting out of the car, he dropped his rake and start walking towards me. Abner also was on the deacon board, but because of his job as a computer salesman, he is out of town a lot. And unfortunately he has been of town when some of these meetings were going on. Plus, Abner is my brother in law. I think the chairman intentionally set a lot of these meetings during the middle of the week to make sure he would not be there.

      "Hey Abner," I said.

      "What's up in law." He responded.

      "I don't know you tell me," I said.

      "Well let's go inside. I think your sister has some not so good news for you."

      "Oh yeah?" I said. Ellen opened the door and gave me a hug.

      "Come on in," she said. "Would you like something to drink? Coffee, Pepsi, juice?"

      "Something smells good." I said. "What's for dinner?"

      "Your favorite, fried chicken. Are you staying?"

      "Oh yes! I'll have a Pepsi with my dinner." We all went into the living room. Ellen yelled back into the kitchen to her middle daughter to keep an eye on the food.

      "What is this news?" I asked.

      "Well, she said, last Sunday, the chairman called an emergency meeting with the church immediately after service. By the way why weren't you there?"

"I was not there because I was not aware of the meeting being held last Sunday. As a matter of fact last Friday evening I met with the deacon board."

"Well, what was that meeting all about?" Ellen asked.

"Just hold on. I'll tell you everything. I am finding it very hard to believe that those snakes met with the church in my absence."

"Well, you know how that chairman is." Ellen said. "He is not satisfied unless he is running the church as he sees fit."

"Ellen, Abner, you all are not going to believe this. I met with the board on last Friday evening. As a matter of fact, I was informed by deacon Jerome Baron about a meeting that the board wanted to have with me. So I showed up last Friday night at the Church. Sure enough, they were all there, except you Abner. As soon as I walked in and took a seat, the meeting got started with no hesitation. Anyway, they gave me an opportunity to talk and to basically explain to them what was really going on. Here is another thing that you won't believe. I was also informed that they had already had a meeting with Eva and she admitted to them that our separation was a mutual agreement. The chairman also wanted me to know that she assured them that in the event the Church decides to retain me, she would not cause any problems."

"Well what about that rumor that she has circulating around the church?" Ellen asked?

"Girl, they didn't question her about the rumor. The chairman proceeded to let me know that the board was not concerned about the rumor. As a matter of fact, he said, we don't even believe what is being said."

"Why then are they trying to prevent you from being retained in the pastor's position if the rumor is not a problem to them?" asked Abner.

"Abner this is what he told me out of his own mouth. The problem that the board has is the possibility of the Church retaining me without being married."

"Well is this a Church policy that they are now trying to enforce?" asked Ellen.

"Not to my knowledge." I said. "I have seen no such policy that has a stated requirement that the pastor of Community Church must be married. Anyway, he basically told me that his pastor has to be a man who is married. So there you have it. There are two snakes now that are slithering around in the Church in an effort to oust me. *Eva's vengeful rumor and the chairman of the board the runner of everything.* So tell me, dear sister, what did he have to say in the meeting with the Church."

"Let me start telling you what I have to tell you by first saying, he gave the Church a bad impression of you." Ellen said.

"How?" I asked.

"Well for starters he opened the floor for a few questions from the congregation. One of the most important question asked was, *"why can't we the Church retained him as our pastor, but give him some time off to iron out his marital situation."* Everybody in the meeting agreed that this is a good suggestion. Mother Hattie Mason stood on her feet to offer a motion that this idea be accepted and acted upon. But before he would carry the motion through, Mr. Chairman proceeded to inform the Church that he didn't think you were interested in coming back. He told them that you told the board when you all met that you were not interested in coming back to the Church, you were not interested in anything that had to do with this Church. And Randall before he made this last statement, he almost had, even me convinced. You know how stubborn you can be at times."

"Yeah Ellen, stubborn but not stupid." I said.

"Anyway," she continued, "when he started telling the Church you were not interested in God or anything that had to do with God, I knew then he was lying. And I jumped up from my seat and told him that this could not be true. Of course, being your sister, all he did was turn and mocked me by saying; of course you will uphold him. He's your brother."

"So tell me, what was the reaction of the Church after that," I asked.

"After he had finished his run down of you, somebody else in the congregation asked if there was a number where you could be reached so that others might try to talk to you. The chairman then tells them, that he tried to call you at the only number that he had, but to no avail."

"That lying, two-faced demon from hell needs to be struck down and cast out of the Church!" I said. "He is really determined to do all that he can to convince the Church that I am not good for them. Even if it means sending his own soul to hell, he is really determined. Do you not know I gave that lying double-tongued menace three telephone numbers before I left the meeting with them. I gave them your number, my work number as well as Darlene's number. He didn't try to call me. Well guess what, I don't need to be pastoring no Church that has a board of deacons that will undermine me like this. So Abner," I said, "has anyone made any attempts to notify you about any of these meetings that have been going on?"

"No." Abner said. "Although they know I am out of town until the weekends, it did not stop them from calling and leaving messages with Ellen about meetings before all of this came up."

"You know why" I said. "You are my brother in law. And they know they would not have been able to accomplish all of the evil deeds against me, as long as you were present."

"Come on Randall; let's get a bite to eat. And listen, don't you be running around here worrying your head off about this mess. As long as you and the Lord know the truth, that's what counts. If it is God's will for you to be back at Community, then you will be back. And if not, then God has something better in store for you, okay."

"Alright Ellen," I said. "I believe you and I trust God to work this thing out for my good. I am quite hungry. I haven't had anything to eat since about lunchtime at work."

"Oh, by the way Randall," Ellen said "last week the music department had a special meeting about a summer concert. Your name came up and it seems as though you still have their support. The president of the department made a suggestion that if you are not retained as pastor they were definitely going to be asking you if you would come back and help keep the music department going."

"I might consider it. As we all know an idea like that will certainly please the board of ruling deacons." I laughed.

CHAPTER XI

GOING BACK TO THE OLD LANDMARK

In spite of all that has been done and said, I woke this morning with such a desire to be in the house of the Lord. Actually my desire was to be back in Community Church. So getting dressed this morning to go to church was a pleasure. As I stepped out of the shower, I could hear the phone ringing and Darlene saying in the background, *"he's in the shower."* So I wrapped a towel around me and dashed out of the bathroom to catch the call before they hung up. *"I'm here."* So Darlene hand tossed me the portable receiver just in time to catch the person on the other end. *"Hello" I said, "this is Randall Whitnall".*

"Good morning Reverend, how are you? Came the voice on the other end. Reverend this is Otis Henley."

"Mr. Henley, how can I help you?"

"Well Brother Whitnall, I was wondering if by chance you were going to Church today and what are your plans after Church?"

"I am most certainly going back to Church today, as a matter of fact, I am in the process of getting dressed now. As for my plans afterwards, I really don't have any, except to come back home for a quiet evening."

"Well Reverend, I would like to get together with you after service and maybe sit down to talk with you about what has been going on and the gossip that has been circulating since you and your wife split up."

"Well Mr. Henley you are quite welcome to come by the apartment at about two-thirty this afternoon. As a matter of fact, I am staying with my sister right now and she is going to be going over to her boyfriend's for the evening. So it will give us an opportunity to really talk about this mess without any distractions."

"What is the address?"

"Oh I'm sorry; the address is 144 Wissahickon Park Apartments, apartment number 14-A. So will you be attending Church this morning, Mr. Henley?"

"Oh no, I won't be going back to Community Church until those folks choose to do the right thing about this situation."

"Well Mr. Henley, I will see you this afternoon when we can talk about all of this nonsense that is causing so much stir in the Church."

I must admit, arriving at the church made me a little nervous. I didn't know how the people would receive me. But this is the Church that I wanted to be in, so here I am. As I drove into the parking lot, other people were arriving at the same time. I chose to go inside from the side entrance thinking I would escape facing most of the people. But to my surprise many going in saw me and followed me into the church. As I turned to go up into the sanctuary deacon Phil Baron stopped me. He asked me to accompany him into the office. I followed him, wandering what demon would I have to battle this morning. After we were both in the office, he closed the door and proceeded to instruct me about what he wanted and what he did not want me to do or say in the Church. He even had the nerve to tell me to make sure I don't say anything that would cause any more confusion. After he finished, I simply looked him straight in the eyes and boldly said to him, "you must be out of your evil mind. I love God and respect his house enough to know how to conduct myself. Furthermore, I said, don't you ever approach me again this way. You are out of order, not to mention being quite disrespectful to me." And then I walked out of the room and left him standing in the room shaking his head with a disgusting, disappointed look on his face.

Service had just begun. The choir had started marching into the loft singing, *"Let's all go back to the Old Landmark."* I followed behind them down to the front of the Church to a seat in the corner that was just waiting for me. As I stood there at my seat, while the choir was singing, I noticed quite a few people nod their heads to me as a sign of their joy to see me again. So I nodded back and gave them a smile of gratitude. I simply could not hold back the tears. I knew I was where I needed to be, if only for just that moment.

Service was just great. The guest speaker they had was really good; he said a lot of things that were rightfully so about the things that were going on in the Church. The chairman seemed as if he did not approve of the things that the minister was saying. After all, the truth hurts sometimes.

Just before the service ended all ministers were given an opportunity say a few words. I was the last one to speak, so naturally all eyes were focused and all hears were opened to hear what I had to say. All I said was, "it's good to be back, I am back to stay and no matter what the devil tries to do, I have the victory." Much to my surprise, I received a standing ovation. And it lasted for about five minutes. As I came down from the podium, I looked over in the corner at the Chairman. His face was beet red with anguish and disappointment. I on the other hand, felt good because I knew that from the response that I had received, there were still some people at Community who appreciated my labor of love. After the service was over, many people came to me and express their desire to see me back at Community as the pastor. One of the mother s of the Church even told me that if by chance I should start another Church, she would definitely leave Community to support me. They all came one by one to me and lifted my spirit with words of encouragement and inspiration. I really needed that.

CHAPTER XII

MEETING WITH THE ACCUSED ACCOMPLICE

    I had to make a quick stop at the grocery store to pick up a bottle or two of soda. It was not quite two-thirty and I assumed Brother Henley would not arrive at the exact time. But to my surprise, as I pulled into the parking lot, I spotted him as he was getting out of his car to go into the apartment building. So I blew my horn, to get his attention. But he just kept right on walking. By the time I got out of the car and headed into the building, he was coming down the steps. "How are you, Mr. Henley?" I asked.

    "Oh, hello Reverend, I am doing good" he replied.

    "Your timing and my arrival are just right. Come on up. Make yourself at home. How long have you been here, I asked?"

    "I've been here only about five minutes." Mr. Henley was seated in the living room, while I poured us both a glass of Pepsi.

    "So how was Church today? Did anybody give you any trouble, he asked?"

    "To tell you the truth, it was a great day. Of course, I had to deal with the devil himself as soon as I stepped inside of the Church."

    "Who was that, he asked?"

    "Man, I'm talking about that lying demon of a human named, Phil Baron."

    "Oh yeah, I heard that he could be a tough one to deal with."

    "Oh believe me, he is no match for me. I simply say what I have to say and that's it. Which is one of the reasons he does not care too much for me. I do not bow down to him and let him run over me as I have seen others do. As a matter of fact, the whole deacon board is under his control. But Certainly we are not here to spend the afternoon talking about him" I said. "So let's get started. What is it you want to talk to me about?"

"Well Reverend, I just wanted to hear from you what is really going on with your wife, the so-called 1st Lady?"

"Your guess is as good as mine," I said. "However, I will tell you this. Her motive is merely revenge."

"Revenge against who and why?" Brother Henley asked.

"Revenge on me, who else? Her husband who so unrighteously dumped her for another man. Unfortunately, you happen to be the man."

"That's another thing I want to know, he said. Why me? Why is she telling everybody that I am the one involved?"

"Listen brother, let me try to make you understand what is really going on. At first, I didn't believe nor could I understand why or what she was doing. You see our separation was a mutual agreement. She even advised me about going before the Church with the truth. Then all of a sudden, after I did what I felt like was the best thing to do, I started hearing about this rumor circulating throughout the Church."

"Have you even tried to talk to her to see where her head is, he asked? Man, when I heard about it, the first thing I did was to approach her. She even admitted that she was the one who started the rumor. And her reason was, basically revenge. But I still was not satisfied until; I received a phone call from your wife asking me to meet with her one day for dinner. So I met her and I must say, I am glad that I did. Because she put the missing piece of the puzzle in place. Which piece was that, Reverend? The truth behind her motive, I said. You see, she was willing and glad for us to go our separate ways. But the thing that set her off was that I moved too quickly for her. Your wife told me all about conversations that the two of them had about both of us. Seems as though she told Eva about an assumption that she had of you and just for the record, it was something that my wife has been using against me for seven years. It happened to have been some information that she could use in the mix of her plot to destroy me. Your wife also told me that my wife had confided in her about her plans to leave me. This was her plan. After she had gotten a new car and a certain amount of money from me, she was going to pack her stuff and walk away without saying a word to me. But because I moved toward the separation before she could get the right amount of money, she got furious and sought revenge by way of a scandal. Now there is the whole story in a nutshell. You know Reverend; I am going to say this to you now that I have heard the whole story. Ever since I came to Community Church, I always felt that there was something strange and phony about Mrs. Whitnall. To me she just appeared to be a fake. I expressed this to my wife several times. But of course, you can imagine what kind of argument that started. After all, my wife thought the sun rose and set with your wife. No offense. Listen brother Otis, there is none taken. Right now I could care less about that wicked woman. My happiness is in knowing, I am no longer sleeping with the enemy. People can say whatever they want to say. What's important to me is, I know the truth, Eva knows the truth and the Lord knows the truth.

So what are you going to do with your life now that you are no longer pastor of the Church, asked brother Henley? And the possibility of your going back as pastor appears to me to be very slim. Well I said I still have my job that I like very much. My son is a bit too young for me to even think that the court would give me custody of him. So I am going to continue living in this town so that I can be close to my son. I also heard from my sister that the music department in Community Church want me to come back to help them if the Church does not retain me as pastor. So that's an option that I might consider.

What about you, I asked? Now that you and your wife are no longer together, what will you be doing? By the way, where are you living now? I also have a good job that I like, stated Otis. So I will remain in this area as long as I have a job. Plus I also have a child that I want to be close by. Right now I am staying with my cousin not too far from here.

Well, summer is just around the corner and now I will have more time to do some of the things that I really enjoy doing. That is fishing, going to yard sales and flee markets. You are welcomed to go with me sometime. Seeing how the rumors have you as my *trusted accomplice*. Yeah, I might as well start living up to my new status in life. We both laughed and then ended the evening with a word of prayer and a firm handshake.

CHAPTER XIII

A SEASON TO SUFFER FOR A SEASON OF BLESSINGS

Twelve years have passed and Otis Henley has become a true friend and brother in the Lord. After all of my other so-called friends walked away from me, not wanting to be on either side of this ugly battle with the devil. Brother Henley along with my sister Ellen, her family and about twelve other people from Community Church, remained faithful in my defense and supported me through all of the storms and times of persecution that I had to go through. Though twelve years have passed, I am in the process of celebrating ten years of successfully pastoring a dynamic ministry and Church that reaches out to people who are hurting, feeling rejected and at times people who are alone and have been deserted. It is in fact a great Church of Deliverance for all people. In these past ten years, as a young Church, I must admit, we have suffered and also endued our sufferings like a much older Church. God alone has tested us and has tried us, as silver is tried. He brought us into the net. He laid afflictions upon our bodies. God caused men to ride over our heads. At times, some of us went through fire and then at times some of us went through floods. And now I can truly say, it is God alone who is able has brought us out into this place and time of wealth and prosperity.

Twelve years ago it look like we were coming in last. But thanks be to our God who is able to deliver us, we are now contending for first place in the kingdom. It is in this twelfth year that God has sent increase into this body. The body is active and well known in the community. The *gossip* that used to circulate has caused many to come and personally witness the *gospel* of Jesus Christ being manifested through the greatest form of love. He has truly prepared a table before me in the presence of my enemies.

One Sunday morning about five years ago, Eva, came walking through the doors to join us in service. The spirit of Lord was moving mightily this particular day. But He moved upon her heart in such a way that it caused her to stand to her feet and confess the sin and apologize for lying on me, brother Henley and others in our congregation. I don't know that she ever confessed in the place where she originally started her destruction, which was in Community Church. Then again I don't know that it would even make a difference if she did. All I know is, *"my cup is running over and I am drinking from my saucer."* And that's good enough for me. One other thing that I do thank God for is that after twelve years of struggling, Eva and I have a good working relationship as it relates to our son, Joshua who is now a very active teenager.

As I look back over all that the Lord has brought me through, I have concluded three important facts of life in the work of the Lord. Number one fact is found recorded in Romans 8:28. *"And we know that all things work together for good to them that love God, to them who are the called according to his purpose."* The second fact of life is found recorded in Philippians 1:6. *"And being confident of this very thing, that he who hath begun a good work in you will perform it until the day of Jesus Christ."* The third and last fact is linked to abundant living as it relates to suffering for the cause of Christ. *"The greater the suffering, the greater the anointing."* If you ever want to be anointed by God, just know that there is a price to pay for this precious anointing.

Finally, my dear friends please understand that the evil deeds of the 1st Lady were allowed by God to take place for my good. I am better than blessed because of her deeds. I have endued as the word of God so states. James 1:12: *"Blessed is the man that endureth temptation; for when he is tested, he shall receive the crown of life which the Lord hath promised to them that love Him."*

Perhaps you may be reading this book and experiencing a great time of trials and persecution. Perhaps you have asked yourself the question, *how will I ever make it through this ordeal? How can I rejoice, how can I walk and hold my head up high as I go through this terrible time?* Well guess what. In the beginning of my ordeal, which by the way lasted a good seven-year, I felt the same way. Disgusted, crushed, bitter, confused and anything else that accompanies a season of hard times. I even remember so vivid reading James 1:2 that says, *"My brethren, count it all joy when you fall into various trials."* Refusing to complete that verse, I began to have a conversation with the Holy Spirit. The first question that I asked was, *"How in the world can anybody have joy going through a trial of this magnitude?"* Well the first response that I receive from the Holy Spirit, or rather the first answer that I got was the word *truth. No the truth and the truth will set you free.* As I began to meditate on the word truth, I realized the importance, the weight, the power that truth has in any situation. Over and against all of the lies and rumors, defamation of my name and reputation, what really is the truth? I finally concluded, until the dust settles and the devil flees, all I have left is the real truth. Only three people in the whole wide world knew the real truth. God, Eva and myself. As I began to focus on the truth of my trial, rather than the rumors and lies, I began to be released and set free from a lot of pain. The first releasing came as began to rebuke the spirit of a false burden. Walking around with my head hung down in shame because Rumors and not reality. You see, the devil does play tricks on your mind. Just as he tricked Eve, in the beginning, in the Garden, he is still doing the same thing. And so as I continued to focus on the truth behind the fall of our marriage, I realized that the devil had me feeling guilty and ashamed because of the effect that these lies had on the people that I cared for so much. People who actually responded to what they had been told, not what they knew as true fact.

Well, after being set free from that false burden, I consulted the spirit one more time. I asked, *"why then am I being subjected to such persecution if the truth has more power than the lies."* Here is what I received as an answer. *"Though the truth is far from the actual rumors, this thing is being done for your good."* Suddenly I was led to Romans 8:28, which reads; *"And we know that all things work together for good to them that love God, to them who are the called according to his purpose."* Dear Sir, dear Ma'am, my joy in the midst of all that I had to go through came when I finally realized that the whole trial was going to work for my good. No I did not know it at first, but I soon realized I was being set up to be blessed by God. If you remember the story of Job, he was baffled by the calamity that came his way. But after assessing the situation, talking to God and reflecting on that which was true about himself and God, he realized that he too had been set up to be royally blessed by God. Though Job was a man who was perfect and upright and feared God, God actually set him up for the purpose of testing and refining his character. There is still room for God to test and refine the character in all of us, no matter how upright we are trying to walk before God. What matters is, God cares enough for us to improve us as He sees fit. When Job finally realized what was going on and why it was going on, he declared; Job 42:46; *"Wherefore I abhor myself and repent in dust and ashes."* You see, the sufferings of Job are actually shown to be corrective rather than penal. Job's friends thought God was punishing him for some sin or sins that he had committed. My friend, the same hold true for believers today. Our trials and troubles are allowed by God to correct some things in us that we may not even be aware of. And so if you are watchful as well as prayerful, the devil, that old deceiver will have you, your friends, your Church members, your family thinking that your suffering is happening because of sin in your life. But here again I serve notice on you to always keep focused on the truth behind the rumors. For truth will set you free every time. Although I could not see it, nor was I able to phantom how any good could possibly come out of my storm, just knowing that I had heard from the Lord that it was going to work for my good made me happy. It is the truth behind my situation, behind your situation that matters. Because whether good or bad, remember, *all things work together for the good of them that love God.* Again, the truth is, what the devil has meant for bad, the Lord is able to turn it around for your good.

One other point I would like to make is, suffering through trials and tribulations really has it rewards. I am a living witness. St. Matthew 5:11-12 says; *"Blessed are ye when men revile you and persecute you and shall say all manner of evil against you falsely, for my sake. Rejoice and be exceedingly glad, for great is your reward in heaven."* In this life, the reward of suffering for the sake of Christ, which is priceless, is the anointing. The greater the suffering for Christ sake, the greater the anointing. Most of us in the body of Christ do desire to be anointed by God for service. As we all know, no service or ministry to God is effective except the anointing, *(or personality of the Holy Spirit)* is involved. And so because of the power and effect that the anointing has we will indeed find ourselves seeking God for a greater anointing. What most of us don't realize is, though God is always willing to bring increase into your service or ministry to Him, He will allow suffering to come as a way of first purging us of all that we need to let go for increase in our life and once we have been purged of our sins, our faults, our bad habits, He will then, through the Holy Spirit, infill and indwell us with a greater anointing.

So cheer up my brother, cheer up my sister: your season of suffering has to come before you walk into your season of blessings. As a matter of fact, your season of suffering will give you a greater appreciation for your season of blessings. Can you imagine what it would be like if we never had to go through anything, if we never had to suffer, be tested, or tried. Our heads would get so big. And none of the glory and honor would we attempt to give to God for our success in life. So instead of wondering and asking yourself the question, why me, go ahead and *accept what God has allowed.* Go ahead and go through your tunnel of despair. Go ahead and face your circumstance with the determination of Ruth. If you remember, great child of God, Ruth was the widowed daughter-in-law of Naomi, who was determined to hold onto her fidelity and loyalty to her mother-in-law. Facing the uncertainties of being a young widow in her days was a great challenge. For as we all know, the social status of women was in way as it is today. Women were definitely and totally dependent upon their husbands, if married, their fathers, if single for their livelihood. After about ten years of being married to Naomi's son, he died and left her alone. *(Ruth 1:4-5)* To make a long story short, Ruth's blessing of being redeemed by Boaz *(Ruth 4:1-16)* came because she was determined not to turn around and go back to her mothers' house. Be encouraged, for the reward of your season of suffering lies ahead of you and not behind you. Press through your storm to the other side. For on the other side awaits your kinsmen redeemer. It is there, on the other side of your storm that Christ awaits to redeem you and reward you for your fidelity and loyalty to him. Be strong and of good courage and He who alone is able to keep you will indeed rescue you. Like the Timex watch slogan, *"take your licking and keep on ticking."*

I am so grateful to God that I did not give up. I did not run away. I did give in to the pressures of my season of suffering. For if I had, I know without a shadow of doubt, I would not have made it to see this time of reward in my life. Finally, my brothers and my sisters in Christ, I encourage you to ride your storm out. I am very much aware of what it feels like when your life is seemingly taking a turn for the worst. But trust me, this storm is only your test. Whatever you do, don't get stuck in your storm because you refuse to face your storm. Speak to your storm. Tell your storm that it won't be long before the sun will shine again. Your storm has come because God is preparing you for the next level in your life. Your storm has come as a tuning fork to fine-tune your character and personality for the Lord. Your storm has come to mature your for the next level of ministry. Simply stand back and see the salvation of the Lord. Give God the opportunity to stand at the helm of your storm and declare, **Peace Be Still**.

THE END